This book is to be returned on or before

The World
is Sweet

The World is Sweet

POEMS BY
Valerie Bloom

ILLUSTRATED BY
Debbie Lush

BLOOMSBURY
CHILDREN'S
BOOKS

First published in Great Britain in 2000
Bloomsbury Publishing Plc, 38 Soho Square, London, W1V 5DF

The moral right of the author has been asserted
A CIP catalogue record of this book is available from the
British Library

ISBN 0 7475 4750 5

Printed in England by Clays Ltd, St Ives plc

10 9 8 7 6 5 4 3 2 1

For Gerry, Ian, Rochelle, Sarah,
David and Pippa

Contents

Frost

Overnight, a giant spilt icing sugar on the ground,
He spilt it on the hedgerows, and the trees without a
    sound,
He made a wedding-cake of the haystack in the field,
He dredged the countryside and the grass was all
    concealed,
He sprinkled sugar on the roofs, in patches not too
    neat,
And in the morning when we woke, the world around
    was sweet.

Seasons

Spring is a baby,
bright, fresh and new,
gurgling with the melting snow,
singing with the first cuckoo.

Summer is a barefoot boy,
fishing in the stream,
running through the waiting corn,
lazing in a dream.

Autumn's a grown man,
slowly walking by,
a limp in his careful footstep,
a shadow in one eye.

Winter is an aged sage,
with long, snow-powdered hair.
He cuts a trench in the frozen ground,
and buries another year.

Next Door's Cat

Next door's cat is by the pond,
Sitting, waiting for the fish,
Next door's cat thinks Geraldine
Would make a tasty dish.

He's had Twinkle and Rose Red,
He ate Alberta too,
And all we found were Junior's bones
When that horrid cat was through.

Next door's cat comes round at night,
Strikes when we're in bed,
In the morning when we wake,
Another fish is dead.

Next door's cat has seen the new fish,
He thinks that it's a goner,
What a surprise he's going to get,
When he finds it's a piranha.

Goldfish

You are trying to tell me something.
I see your mouth open and close,
An O sad as tears,
But I hear only the silence,
And an occasional apostrophe
Of despair.

The Old House

They say, in the night when the dogs take fright
And run howling from the streets,
When the hooded owl shrieks, and the wild wind
   wails,
And you lie shaking beneath the sheets,

They say, when the moon is too terrified
To play with the stones in the drive,
When bats bury their heads beneath their wings,
Then the old house comes alive.

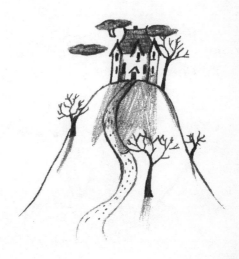

He came from a place near the sunset,
He went to a place without light,
He walked too late without company,
He walked too late at night.

He could have come early, at six or seven,
Or even later, at four or five,
But he chose to arrive at the very hour
That the old house came alive.

He heard that old house calling,
He had no power to say no,
He climbed up the hill, crossed over the bridge,
Though he knew that he shouldn't go.

Its voice was like a lost child's,
Soft and plaintive in the breeze,
It spoke of the pain it was feeling
That only he could ease.

It whispered to him in strange words
That no one else could hear,
Weird words that held such promises,
That would fill sane men with fear.

His head urgently whispered a caution,
'You'll turn back now if you are smart'.
But he had no will to listen,
For the house had hold of his heart.

He stepped on to the porch where the rotting boards
    creaked,
Through the door that beckoned, ajar,
Towards a light that flickered and peaked
Like a single, lonely star.

He heard the creaking door slam shut,
The festering floorboards sigh,
As in a dream, he thought, 'How sad,
I've come this far to die.'

They heard the scream, felt the anguish,
They knew he would not survive,
And they hear it still every night at twelve
When the old house comes alive.

Scared of the Dark

I'm scared of the dark
I don't like it one bit,
I'm scared of the dark,
There, I've admitted it.

I'm scared of the things
That go bump in the night
I'm scared of the creatures
Outside of the light.

I'm scared of the dark,
And what scares me the most,
Is when in the dark
I meet another ghost.

Jeremy Bishop

Jeremy, Jeremy Bishop,
Was a good boy, he ate all his fishop,
When he was done,
Like a well-brought up son,
He washed and dried his dishop.

My Brother Helps Out

Can I help you make the cake, Mum?
Please, let me, I know how,
I can do it, ple-ee-ee-ze! Oh thank you!
Let me have it. Right. What now?

Oh yes, I knew that, this is easy,
I'll be careful, I won't hurry,
Whisk it like this, right? I'm okay,
Honest I can do – oops! sorry.

Can I help you clean the windows?
Can I use the Windolene?
I'll not smudge it, I can do it,
C'mon, Mum, please, don't be mean.

Oh yes, I knew that, leave me to it,
I'll be careful, don't you worry,
Spray it like this, right? I'm all right,
Yes I'll mind your eyes – oops! sorry.

Can I help you mop the floor, Mum?
I have mopped the floor before,
Let me do it, 'cause I know that
You think mopping is a chore.

I'll be careful with the bucket,
There's no need for such a flurry,
Don't you trust me? I'll just put
The bucket on this stool – oops! sorry.

Are you making bread-rolls, Lucy?
Can I help you knead the dough?
I am nearly as old as you now,
So can I help you? Can I?
NO!

My Sister Tells a Joke

There was this man . . .
Now tell me if you've heard this one before.
Please Jonathan, come away from the bedroom door.

There was this man . . .
Or was it a boy? Doesn't really matter, I suppose,
Oh, Rachael! You shouldn't punch Jonathan on the
    nose!

There was this man . . .
Jonathan, I'm sure she didn't mean any harm.
Yes, Rachael, I remembered to set the alarm.

There was this man . . .
Rachael, you can't play that tape again!
Jon, what are you doing? Give me that fountain pen.

There was this man . . .
Will you two please listen to me!
That's better. Now where was I? Let me see

There was this man . . .
Hold on a minute; let me make sure I get this right,
Oh bother, here's Mum, come to turn out the light.

Rachael, here's your tape, Jonathan, take your pen,
Remind me never to try and tell you two a joke again.

Guidance

Wash yuh han' dem before yuh eat,
Sit still, teck yuh foot dem off the seat,
Don' scrape the plate with yuh knife an' fork,
An' keep quiet when big people a-talk,
Stop drag yuh foot dem pon the floor,
Ah tell yuh a'ready, don' slam the door,
Cover up yuh mout' when yuh a-cough,
Don' be greedy, give yuh sister half
O' the banana that yuh eatin' there,
What kind o' dress that yuh a-wear?
Don' kiss yuh teeth when me talk to yuh,
An' mind how yuh lookin' at me too,
Teck me good advice, me girl,
Manners carry yuh through the worl',
Ah tellin' yuh all this fe yuh own good,
Yuh should thank me, show some gratitude.

Life is very tough for me,
When Uncle Henry comes to tea.

Next Door's Cat – 2

Next door's cat ate my piranha,
He ate it for a lark,
I've put a new fish in the pond,
And this time it's a shark.

Something Comes

Over the mountains,
Like thunder of drums,
Shaking the leaves from trees,
Something comes.

Down through the valleys
With the bellow of bombs,
Alarming the cows and sheep,
Something comes.

Up through the forests,
The frightened air hums,
For tearing it in pieces,
Something comes.

Moving up the driveway
With a noise that numbs,
Crumpling the paving stones
Something COMES!

We Don't Believe

We don't believe in ghosts, Child,
We don't believe in ghosts,
We don't believe in goblins, ghouls,
Or any of the hosts

Of weird creatures you read about,
In comics and fairy tales,
We don't believe in things with fangs,
Sharp claws and pointed tails

Which are said to visit folk asleep,
And steal babies away,
We don't believe in changelings,
Or trolls that force you to obey

Their many evil wishes,
Who can bind you to their will,
We don't believe in leprechauns,
And we don't believe there's a hill

Where lords and ladies dance all night,
And disappear at dawn,
We don't believe in the naiad,
The dryad, or the faun

Who lurk in streams and forest trees,
Or fearsome creatures of the night,
We don't believe in vampires
Who creep inside and bite

You when you're sleeping,
And suck you dry of blood,
We don't believe in children
Living in a wood

Whose feet are turned behind them,
And whose piteous calls
Will slyly lure you to your death.
We don't believe in walls

Covered in moss and lichen,
Concealing magic doors,
We don't believe in fairy folk
Living beneath your floors

Who crawl through your rooms after dark,
Who turn the fresh milk sour,
And we certainly do not believe
In the supernatural power

Of werewolves, zombies, dragons,
Or in houses that are cursed,
There's nothing in the cellar, Child,
So come on! . . . You go first.

Snake

Sneaky Mr.
Forked tongue Twr.
Caught my Sr.
When he Kr.
Gave her a Blr.

How to Ask for a Hamster
(for Tamara)

Mum, can I keep a snake in my room?
What did you say? Are you mad?
Well, Jamie keeps a snake in *his* room,
He got it from his dad.

Will you buy me a mongoose, Mum?
I've played with one; it belongs to Maria,
It's really docile, can I please, Mum?
I don't think that's a good idea!

Can I have a pony then?
I could afford to pay for hay.
D 'you know how much a pony costs?
Japhet got one for *his* birthday.

How about a crocodile?
They sell them in Didcot.
I think that's where Chloe bought hers.
Can I have one? *Certainly NOT!*

I'll settle for a tarantula then,
It would be in a cage, of course.
Joshua has a tarantula.
Oh no! I can think of nothing worse!

What about a little monkey?
Tina has a chimpanzee.
Everyone in class has a pet,
Everybody except me.

You can have a cat, or a hamster,
You cannot have a snake or mouse.
No crocs, monkey or creepy-crawlies
I won't have a zoo in this house.

Okay, I'll settle for a hamster,
It's better than nothing I suppose.
Oh, there's the doorbell, must be Jamie,
We promised to go and play at Joe's.

Jamie, you were right, I tried it,
Just like you said, it worked a treat,
I'm getting the hamster, now tell me,
How do I ask for a parakeet?

The Plight of the Bumblebee

I can't make honey any more,
I've given up tasting nectar,
Yesterday I lost my job
As chief pollen collector.

I've done with flying from flower to flower,
Given up smelling the rose,
The perfume from the hyacinth
Now just gets up my nose.

I've just been expelled from the hive,
And I'm going now to pack,
The queen said that they don't need me,
There's something that I lack.

It's not my sting, my stripe, my wing,
Which makes me an underachiever,
The thing that's really hampering me,
Is that I've got hay fever.

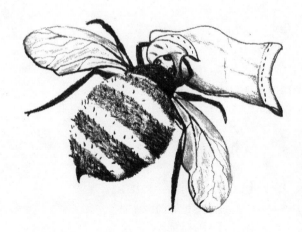

Al Caprawn

He was the meanest marine creature
That ever was seaborne,
Sharp as razors were the claws
Of the fearsome Al Caprawn.

How the little fishes feared him,
How the shivers shook the frame
Of the shark, and how he whimpered
When he heard Al Caprawn's name.

Al Caprawn, Al Caprawn,
He's a gangster, he's a con,
You just know when he's around,
There's something fishy going on.

With pincers brightly flashing,
He paraded 'cross the sand,
Wreaking havoc with the smoking
Water pistol in his hand.

Once he grabbed the giant squid,
Squeezed it dry and stole its ink,
Then he marketed the liquid as
A brand new health food drink.

Al Caprawn, Al Caprawn,
He's a gangster, he's a con,
You just know when he's around,
There's something fishy going on.

With his henchmen Shrimp the Wimp,
Crab the Claw, and Lobster Reds,
He mugged the oysters, stole their pearls
Left them crying in their beds.

The news rocked the whole ocean,
As it went through the grapevine,
Only Al could do this wicked deed,
And on St. Valentine's.

Al Caprawn, Al Caprawn,
He's a gangster, he's a con,
You just know when he's around,
There's something fishy going on.

As a warning to the coral,
Al Caprawn once wrecked their reef,
Told them all, 'Pay me pwotection,
Or you're sure to come to gwief.'

'Hide your moustache,' sobbed the walrus,
'Watch your blubber,' moaned the whale,
'He's an evil little shellfish,
From his pincers to his tail.'

Al Caprawn, Al Caprawn,
He's a gangster, he's a con,
You just know when he's around,
There's something fishy going on.

Like Napoleon and Hitler,
Al got too big for his boots,
He spied a fishing trawler
And set off in hot pursuit.

Then he shouted to the trawler,
'You doity wat, give up that catch!
I will make you vewy sowy
That you twespassed on my patch.'

Al Caprawn, Al Caprawn,
He's a gangster, he's a con,
You just know when he's around,
There's something fishy going on.

'Those fish awe mine!' he bellowed.
'You'll be sowy you were bawn,
I'll teach you not to double-cwoss
The famous Al Capwawn.'

What a lesson to us all,
Not to act before we think,
Al in half an avocado
With a dressing that was PINK!

Al Caprawn, Al Caprawn,
He's a gangster, he's a con,
You just know when he's around,
There's something fishy going on.

Next Door's Cat – 3

Next door's cat ate my shark,
Though it took him quite a while,
So I've stocked the pond with something else,
A cunning crocodile.

The Tall Ships

I saw three ships, three tall ships,
Riding on the sea,
The waves quaked, and the fishes quaked,
And the wind sighed sorrowfully,
For on their decks, and in their holds,
Rode doom and misery.

I saw three ships, three tall ships
Anchored on the sea,
The wind refused to fill the sails,
The sky wept copiously,
For the berths were filled with pain and tears
And they hunted a new country.

I saw three ships, three tall ships
Speed shoreward from the sea,
And the trees moaned, and the birds fled,
And the land cried woefully,
For on their prows sat greed and shame,
And the death of history.

A Town Called Glory

Does the sun still shine on Glory,
Its warm rays still heat the soil,
Paint the rooftops with gold brushes
And make the tarmac boil?

Yes, the sun still shines on Glory,
And it still warms up the land,
And it makes the rooftops sparkle,
As it does the yellow sand.

And the stream that runs through Glory,
Does it sing as soft, as sweet?
And the fish and crabs that swim there,
Are they just as good to eat?

Oh the stream still flows through Glory,
But its song is slow and sad,
The fish and crabs still swim about,
But no one eats them, lad.

Do the fields ripen in Glory,
Do sweet corns and pumpkins grow?
Do the plums and cherries blossom
Side by side and row by row?

Yes, the crops are ripe in Glory,
Though they're not gathered now,
Fruits and vegetables flourish,
But I cannot tell you how.

Do the travellers stop by Glory,
Buy food in the marketplace?
And do strangers still leave Glory,
A broad smile upon each face?

Yes the travellers pass through Glory,
But they do not linger long,
And Glory's praises fall no more
Like manna from the tongue.

Does Old John still tend his cattle
On the hill behind the town?
And does Mary go to meet him
When the sun is going down?

There's a dark cloud on the hilltop
Where Old John once had his herd,
An old man roams the hill at night,
But he doesn't say a word.

A woman goes to meet him,
As the sun is going down,
Each day there's a new sorrow
In this poor, wretched town.

Cropover

There's a smell of burning in the air,
It's cropover, cropover,
It's August and this time of year
It's cropover, cropover,
The canefields have been reaped and there's
Just stubble in the places where
The cane leaves once waved in the air,
It's cropover.

There's a sound of music in the breeze,
It's cropover, cropover,
The drums shout BOOM! And the bamboos wheeze,
It's cropover, cropover,
The dancers leap, lunge, hug and squeeze,
Then pirouette with careless ease,
Cheers cascade from the tops of trees,
It's cropover.

Costumes sparkle in a halogen sun
It's cropover, cropover,
There's playing now the harvest's done,
It's cropover, cropover,
It's night, the feasting has begun,
Those pots of food must weigh a ton,
Now we will have some serious fun,
It's cropover.

Grandma, Bandana, an' Me

Mama tell me 'bout me Nana,
Granny Anna from Guyana.
'She's de sweetest, kindest Nana
That a person ever had,
But one thing about you Nana,
She just mad about bandana,
And the way she wear bandana
Is enough to drive you mad.

Bandana blouse, bandana skirt,
Bandana hat, bandana shoes,
Bandana bag, bandana socks,
A pure bandana Nana use.

Everybody know de custom,
An' is one dem hol' with pride,
White is the usual colour
That they use to dress de bride,
When you granny gettin' married,
People nearly dead with shock,
See her waltzing down de aisle,
In a long bandana frock.

Bandana veil, bandana train,
Bandana sandals, an' bouquet,
When him turn aroun' an see her,
Grandad nearly pass away.'

When ah go to Granny house,
As ah walk in though de door,
All me see was de bandana,
From de ceiling to de floor,
Bandana curtain pon de window,
De same cover pon de chair,
Bandana bedspread pon her bed,
She have bandana everywhere.

Bandana dishcloth in de kitchen,
An' de apron roun' her wais'
Bandana towel in de bathroom,
Granny's a bandana case.

She say to me, 'Ah have a present
Ah been savin' here fe yuh.'
She take out a bandana square an say,
'Now try this on Dudu.
You can tie it in a circle,'
(An she do it with a smile),
'You can leave a little hangin',
Now dat is the lates' style.'

Well ah look into de mirror,
An me heart just miss a beat,
De bandana pon me head look so
Beautiful an' neat,
Ah say, 'Granny ah look pretty!'
But she wasn' satisfy,
So the next time we go shopping,
Granny Anna meck me buy

Bandana skirt, bandana blouse,
Bandana hat, bandana boot,
Ah even buy meself a nice little
Bandana bathing suit.

She say, 'This is jus' the manner
That they dress in ole Guyana,
When my great gran was a girl,' an' ah
Believe her, I suppose,
So now when me go Guyana,
See me an me Granny Anna,
Lookin' like two walkin' banner,
In we bright bandana clothes.

Bandana blouse, bandana skirt,
Bandana hat, bandana shoes,
If you see we in the market,
Is bandana we a choose.

Baffled Turkey

Last night they brought a tree home,
They took it into the hall,
Now why would they do a thing like that?
I don't understand it at all.

Now they're hanging some tinsel upon it,
Some coloured streamers and balls,
And long loopy ribbons of twinkling lights,
I don't understand it at all.

There's a red and green circle on the front door,
And mistletoe on the wall,
And the farmer's inspecting a red and white suit,
I don't understand it at all.

Out on the porch they're erecting
What looks like a manger and stall,
With a stuffed donkey, a baby, and three kings,
I don't understand it at all.

Lately they've given me so much to eat,
I'm almost as round as a ball,
And now they are taking me up to the house,
I don't understand it, at all.

The Old Year's Lament

In January when I was young,
They made a fuss of me,
They welcomed me with singing,
Dancing and revelry.

On the first they celebrated
With a national holiday,
They yelled and cheered when I stepped in,
Shouted, 'Hip, hip, hooray!'

Everyone called me happy
As long as I was new,
And made long lists of all the things
That I would help them do.

And for the twelve months I was with them,
They let me hold their dreams,
I was the overseer,
Of countless plots and schemes.

It's true some lost their loved ones,
While I was in control,
But I tried to keep everyone happy,
And succeeded on the whole.

For those who loved excitement,
And violence, there was war,
Earthquakes, volcanoes, famine,
They couldn't ask for more.

And those who liked a quiet life,
Who preferred ennui,
I gave them those test matches,
And of course, daytime TV

I'm telling you, this human race
Is a very fickle lot,
They've heard the New Year's coming,
A fresh-faced, mewling brat.

They are planning the same celebrations,
We shared not long ago,
And not a single soul it seems
Is sad to see me go.

Secret

Can you keep a secret?
Keep it in your mind,
Don't laugh, don't talk,
Don't write it anywhere
In pen or chalk.

Ah tell me friend a secret,
Ah tell her not to tell,
Ah say is a special secret
So mek sure you keep it well.

Ah know dat it exciting,
But I asking you to try,
It would be bad if it get out,
So cross you heart and hope to die.

So ah tell me friend me secret,
From beginning to de end,
And that was de last o' dat secret,
She didn' even pretend

To keep it safe, she shout out,
In her loudes' voice,
'You mean you like that Malcolm?'
Now you tell me if dat nice?

She say she couldn' help it,
Say ah teck her by surprise,
Say ah really shoulda warn her.
Ah don't like to criticise

But when a person promise,
Take a oath right to your face,
She no ha' no right to broadcast
You business 'bout de place.

So ah ask me mum this morning,
Who can keep a secret most?
And she tell me, so me best friend
From now on is me bedpost.

Next Door's Cat – 4

Next door's cat finished my croc,
Yesterday at three,
I think that cat's a tiger,
And now it's after me.

Black Widow

I hear there's a spider wot eats 'er 'usband
I think that's well bad,
I'm glad I'm not a spider,
I wouldn't like mum to eat dad.

Sandwich

We goin' on a school trip today,
De whole class goin' to Whitney Bay,
Ah teckin' me ball an' bat with me
To play beach cricket, an' let me see,
Ah mustn't forget me new frisbee,
An teacher say to bring a sandwich.

She say to bring a waterproof mac,
An' a change o' clothes in a knapsack,
For it bound to rain, she guarantee,
An' half o' we gwine end up in the sea,
An' we mustn't forget, any o' we,
Teacher say, to bring a sandwich.

She say we can bring a can o' drink,
Ah will bring some fizzy orange, ah think,
Some gobstoppers ah can share with Lee,
(An' everybody else, probably)
An apple or orange, an, ah definitely
Won't forget to bring a sandwich.

Ah ask me mother for some bread,
Some butter, lettuce, an' some ched-
dar cheese, don't need nothing more,
An' ah just headin' for the door
When ah bump into me Granny Lenore,
An' she teck away me sandwich.

She say, don't know what you mother thinkin' 'bout,
How she could let a growin' child go out
With one little sandwich alone to eat,
But don't you worry, chile, in this basket,
I have corn pone, chicken an' jerk meat,
You don't need to teck a sandwich.

Ah say to her, you don't understan',
Ah cannot teck all of dem things, Gran,
De whole o' de class will laugh at me,
She say, I do you favourite fricassee,
Ah tell her, Gran, teacher specifickly
Say dat we must bring a sandwich.

But she not listening to a thing
Me say. She waltz pass me an' den she bring
Out a bowl o' rice an' peas,
A whole hardo bread, if you please,
Ah was down on the floor, pon me hands an' knees
Beggin', give me back me sandwich.

Den Gran teck out a thermos flask,
Ah shut me yeye, ah fraid to ask,
But ah wonder what next she woulda produce,
She say, look, some nice soursop juice,
So gimme dat fizzy nonsense, dat's no use,
And she teck it, jus like me sandwich.

Gran, yuh have enough to feed de whole class dere,
She say, dat is right, yuh must learn to share,
Ah put something in for you teacher too,
And she pull out a bowl o' callaloo,
Ah ax meself, what ah going to do?
Ah only want to teck a sandwich.

No matter how me beg an' plead,
She was like a mad bull on stampede,
So wid chicken, rice an' hardo bread,
Me heart an' foot dem heavy like lead,
Ah wave goodbye to me street cred,
An lef' without me sandwich.

All day ah try to pretend
Ah didn' know dat basket, but in the end
Lunch time come an we all gather roun',
Spread some blanket on the groun'
An everybody settle down,
To open up dem sandwich.

Teacher say, 'What have you got there?'
Ah pretend ah didn' hear,
But dat basket wouldn' go away,
So ah open it an' start to pray
Dat they wouldn' laugh too loud when ah display
What ah bring instead o' sandwich.

Well everybody yeye dem near pop out,
My friend Lee start to lick him mout',
So ah ask dem if dey all want some,
Dey look pon me like ah really dumb,
In no time we finish every crumb,
An dem all feget dem sandwich.

When teacher say, 'Thank your grandmother for us',
Ah feel so proud, ah nearly bus',
She say, 'That was a really super meal,'
Everybody say, 'Yeah, that was well cool, Neil',
An' yuh don' know how glad ah feel
Dat ah didn' bring – a sandwich.

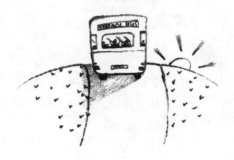

Eat Your Veg

Go on, try the artichoke,
Yes I agree they look
A bit unappetising,
But that TV cook

That you like, gave us the recipe,
And it doesn't taste too bad,
Well how about the peas then?
They're the best *I've* ever had.

What do you mean onions and peppers,
Are too crunchy when you chew?
That's the lamest excuse ever,
Just try a piece . . . won't you?

These tomatoes are full of vitamins,
Oh yes, you hate the seeds,
Will you taste the aubergine?
Then how about some swedes?

Daddy's done these parsnips specially,
Would you like a wedge?
Oh, come on, don't be difficult,
Mummy, eat your veg.

Just Wait

Ah goin' to live in a de forest,
Just meself an' me,
Ah goin' to run away when it get light,
Just you wait an' see.

Nobody goin' be there to tell me
Not to paint me toenail red,
Which dress, or blouse, or skirt to wear,
Or what time to go to bed.

Nobody goin' be there to criticise,
Ah goin' be on me own,
Nobody to frown an' make a fuss,
To groan an' gripe an' moan.

Me chair goin' to be a tree stump,
Me bed, banana trash,
Ah goin' eat me food out o' cocoa leaf,
Drink from a calabash.

Ah goin' brush me teeth with chew stick,
An' wash me face with dew,
Ah goin' use withes to make ribbon,
An' coconut husk make shoes.

Ah goin' swim like turtle in the river,
Swing from the highes' tree,
In fact, ah think ah goin' go right now.

But first, let me see what on TV.

Two Seasons

We don' have a Springtime like some folk
Who live in dem colder place,
but we have a time when de soft rain come,
an' tease open de seedcase
o' de poincianna and de trumpet tree,
An' whisper to de young cane to wake
when de guangu blossom is pink an' white
powder-puff, prettying up de earth face.
But not Spring like in dem colder place.

We no have no Summer when Springtime done,
no change o' season as such,
but we have a time when de asphalt bubble
in de hot sun, when yuh dare not touch
de tarmac wid yuh barefoot; when de heat is
a dancin' dervish who wi' grab yuh
an' spin yuh till de sweat is a river flowin' down,
an' yuh too tired fe do anything much.
But we don' have a summer as such.

We no have no Autumn like Europe,
we don' have de American Fall,
but dere is a time when de flame tree in the Forest
light de woodland like a fireball,
when de blue mahoe leaf dem turn bright bronze,
de almond look like it wearing henna,
when de nightfall flicker wid peeni-wallie,
an' grasshopper an' tree-frog call
to de moon. But we don' have Autumn nor Fall.

We don' have no winter wid snow an' sleet,
an ice like a carpet pon de grung,
but we have a time when de fee-fee twist
purple an' white up de road bank, an' young
tangerine an' ugli fruit swell an' yellow in
de gentle sun; when de cool breeze finger
draw de sweater round de shoulder,
an de sorrel tas'e tart pon de tongue.
But no ice like a carpet pon de grung.

We don't have de four season dem,
Summer, Winter, Autumn an' Spring,
but de dry season wid the noisy bees
an' de shrill call o' de cling-cling,
an' de sun turnin' de sea into a hot bath,
an' de grass bake so dat it crackle like parchment
under yuh foot; when de beach dem crowded
wid folk cooling off; de season when mango is king.
But not Summer, Winter, Autumn an' Spring.

No, we don't have four different season,
just two, de wet an' de dry,
an' in de rainy season de storm cloud dem
cover over de face o' de sky,
de road an' de river dem lose dem bank,
an' de hurricane dem sometimes come callin'
fe borrow de roof an' fe tear up de tree dem
like paper. But de earth always revive by an' by,
in de two season, de wet an' de dry.

A Tree Felled

Yesterday he was majestic,
Challenging the sky,
A crown of leaves, emerald green,
Strong limbs to hold the canopy.
Now those leaves lie dry and brittle,
Withered in the sun,
The branches that were arms outstretched,
Lopped, bundled up and gone.
The mighty trunk, a century wide,
Is prone, powerless, compliant,
There is no sadder sight, I think,
Than a broken, fallen giant.

Time

Time's a bird, which leaves its footprints
At the corners of your eyes,
Time's a jockey, racing horses,
The sun and moon across the skies.
Time's a thief, stealing your beauty,
Leaving you with tears and sighs,
But you waste time trying to catch him,
Time's a bird and Time just flies.

Total Eclipse

An eerie light haloes the treetops,
The nightingale ceases to sing,
The owl's eyes open, dilated,
Starlings tuck their heads under their wings.

A cold wind awakes from the waters,
Walks mournfully over the sand,
And the darkness, swift as a flash flood,
Covers the face of the land.

The earth holds its breath in wonder,
The silence complete, unbroken,
And there's a tiny glimpse of the way it was
Before the world was spoken.

Whose Dem Boots

Whose dem boots ah hearin', chile,
Whose dem boots ah hear?
Whose dem boots ah hearin', chile,
Whose dem boots ah hear?
Dem boots trampin' down de road
Dat fill me heart wid fear?

Gotta fin' me a hid'n place,
Whai! Whai!
Gotta fin' me a hid'n place.

Whose dem boots ah hearin', chile,
Comin' thru me gate?
Whose dem boots ah hearin', chile,
Comin' thru me gate?
Trampin' straight up to me door?
Tell dem please to wait.

Gotta fin' me a hid'n place,
Whai! Whai!
Gotta fin' me a hid'n place.

Whose dem boots ah seein', chile,
Stand'n by me bed?
Whose dem boots ah seein', chile,
Stand'n by me bed?
Waitin' dere so patient, chile?
Tell dem go ahead.

Gotta fin' me a hid'n place,
Whai! Whai!
Gotta fin' me a hid'n . . . Huh!

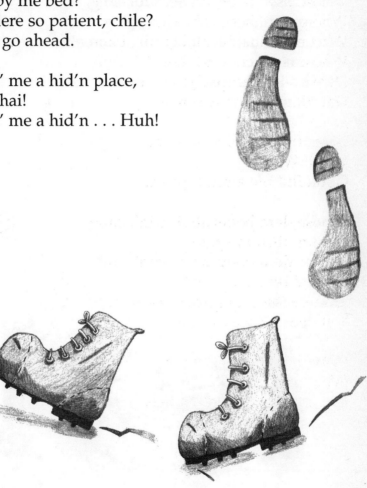

Silence

No grasses whisper, no birds sing,
No sound from any living thing,
No brooks babble, no branches creak,
No hunters cry, no victims shriek,
No dry leaves rustle, no creepies crawl,
There is no sound in the world at all.

Uncle Sam

Uncle Sam is six foot six,
Uncle Sam real brave,
When dem see him comin'
All de bad pickney dem behave.

Uncle Sam a expert
Pon ju-jitsu an' kung fu,
An' wrestlin' an' karate,
Nearly everyt'ing him can do.

Uncle Sam nuh fraid nobody,
Yuh cyaan scare him wid stick or gun,
But when him see a patoo,
Yuh fe see Uncle Sam run!

Mummy, are You Blind?

Mummy, please! For goodness sake,
You just stepped on my wedding cake!
No, that was not a pile of sand.
Oh! Now you've wrecked my new rock band.
They might have looked like three dead flies,
But that's 'cause you're looking with Mummy eyes.
Mum, don't sit there! Be careful, please,
You almost squashed the biscuits and cheese.
What do you mean it's an empty chair?
Anyone could see that's a table there.
Aren't you going to say hello to Sue?
She's standing right there beside you.
Here's your chocolate cake, hope you enjoy it.
Mum, it just *looks* like a dog biscuit.
Oh, Mummy, that's not Rover's bowl,
It's the golden platter that the prince stole
From the giant king. Oh, never mind,
You can go now. It was very kind
Of you to offer to play with me,
But I think I'll just have Sue for tea.
You'd better go and have your dip,
Don't step on my sailing! . . . ship.

Why are grown-ups all so dim?
You have to teach them everything.

I Think Shushila Likes Me

I think Shushila likes me,
My little dove! I'm almost sure.

What do you mean she likes you?
She just showed you to the door!
Yesterday at break time
She whacked you on the head,
You asked her for a kiss,
She gave you a thump instead.
And when you sat in English class
And wrote her that long note,
She laughed loud when she got it
Told the whole class what you wrote.
The names Shushila calls you,
Would make a grown man weep,
She thinks you are a 'reptile',
A 'wimp', a 'jerk', a 'creep'
You think Shushila likes you?
That she is your 'little Dove'?

You're right, she doesn't like me.
That is not like, that's love!

I Hope Tomorrow Never Comes

I don't want to leave today,
Don't want to go tomorrow,
Has anyone got some extra hours?
I want a few to borrow

To add on to the end of today,
For today has been so good,
I cannot bear to have it go,
I'd bottle it if I could.

Then I could keep for ever
My fabulous birthday cake,
The party, the walk this morning,
The hedgehog and grass snake

At the bottom of the garden,
The new baby fishes in the pond,
The game of chess with my dad,
(For the first time I didn't come second).

Today has been so special,
How can I keep it here?
Perhaps if I don't go to sleep
Today won't disappear.

Of all the days I can remember,
Today has been the best,
But all that's waiting in tomorrow
Is another history test.

Goodbye (Cinquain)

And so
as evening falls
I close the curtains on
the empty bed. And shadows creep
inside.

Last Lick

Sue and me walk home from school together every
    day,
We play 'teacher' and 'hide an' seek', and 'tag' along
    the way,
But the best game is the one we always leave until the
    end,
Till just before we reach her gate, right beside the
    double bend.
Sue always get me first, but she won't get me today.
So as she reaching out her hand, I jump out of the way,
Then before she know, I stretch out my hand and
    touch her quick,
And as I racing down the road, I holler out 'LAST
    LICK!'

Glossary

ah	I
ax	ask
banana trash	the dried bark and leaves of the banana tree
callaloo	a leafy vegetable used like spinach; a stew made of callaloo, meats and seasoning
chew-stick	a vine containing a natural cleaning agent, chewed and used by hikers, campers etc as a toothpaste and toothbrush
cling-cling	small bird named after the sound of its call
cropover	the festival which is traditionally held to celebrate the end of the sugar cane harvest in Barbados
cyaan	can't; cannot
dat	that
de	the
dem	they; them; used to denote the plural forms of words e.g. 'han' dem' (hands), 'foot dem' (feet)
den	then
dey	they
don'	don't
fe	for; to

fee-fee	a vine which flowers around Christmas time. The purple and white flowers are partially dismantled and sucked by children to produce a whistling sound
feget	forget; forgot
grung	ground
guangu	a large tree with flowers resembling small pink and white pom-poms
ha'	have
last lick	a game played by children in the Caribbean. The aim is to give the last touch before you say goodbye for the day. A lick in Jamaica is a smack/hit or in this case a touch
mek	make; let
nuh	not; don't
patoo	owl. The owl is believed by some to be an evil omen, its hoot signifying death
peenie-wallie	fireflies
pickney	child
pon	on; upon
tas'e	taste
teck/teckin'	take/taking
trumpet tree	a large tree with seed pods up to sixty-one centimetres (twenty-four inches) long. These pods make a sound like a trumpet when blown.
wi'	will

wid	with
worl'	world
yeye	eye
yuh	you; your

YET MORE POETRY WITH PUNCH FROM BLOOMSBURY CHILDREN'S BOOKS . . .

ISBN 0 7475 4417 4

ISBN 0 7475 4745 9

ISBN 0 7475 4028 4

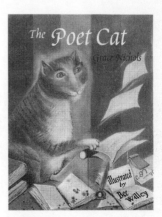

ISBN 0 7475 5064 6

AND MORE . . .

ISBN 0 7475 3866 2

ISBN 0 7475 3864 6

ISBN 0 7475 3863 8

ISBN 0 7475 3865 4

AND MORE . . .!

ISBN 0 7475 4755 6

ISBN 0 7475 4760 2

ISBN 0 7475 4451 4

ISBN 0 7475 4486 7